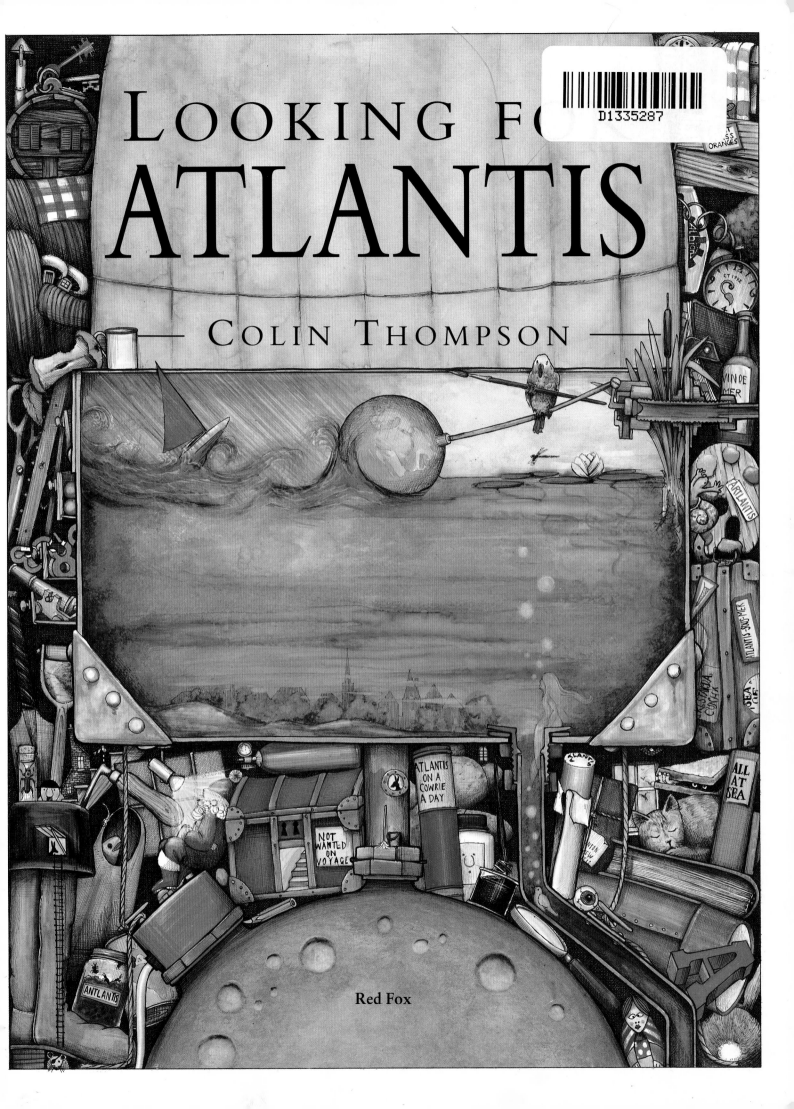

LOOKING FOR ATLANTIS

— COLIN THOMPSON —

Red Fox

For Anne

A Red Fox Book

Published by Random House Children's Books
20 Vauxhall Bridge Road, London SW1V 2SA

A division of Random House UK Ltd.
London Melbourne Sydney Auckland
Johannesburg and agencies throughout the world

First published by Julia MacRae 1993

Red Fox edition 1996

Printed in Singapore

RANDOM HOUSE UK Limited Reg. No. 954009

ISBN 0 09 964521 1

For most of his life my grandfather was away at sea. He sailed across every ocean a hundred times and travelled through every country of the world from the plains of Patagonia to the distant volcano of Tristan da Cunha. He had seven wives and eleven children, was a prince and a pirate, lived with kings and queens and ate off plates of solid gold.

When I was ten and Grandfather was very very old he came home. As autumn arrived and the leaves began to fade he climbed into bed and sat for days, looking out over the harbour towards the faint horizon. At the top of the bed his parrot Titanic fell silent and began to moult. Beside the bed everything he had collected through his long life was packed into a large wooden chest.

"It's for you," he said to me. "Everything you could ever want is in that chest if you know where to look for it."

"I want you to be well again, Grandfather," I said.

"I will be," he said, closing his eyes, "when you get to Atlantis."

"I thought Atlantis was just a story."

"That's only narrow-minded people talking. They wouldn't believe in it if you led them down the main street," he said. "All you have to do is look in the right place."

"But I'm only ten, Grandfather. They won't let me go anywhere."

"Atlantis is right here, all around you," he said. "You have to learn how to look for it."

The old man seemed to sink deep into the pillows as if part of him had drifted away to another place. The room fell completely silent like a bubble floating far above the moon. The autumn sun sat on the roof tops and the whole town looked as if it was made of gold. As the light faded Grandfather set out on his final voyage across a sea of dreams and grey feathers.

"Hello, sailor," said Titanic, and looked away so no one would see the sadness in his eyes.

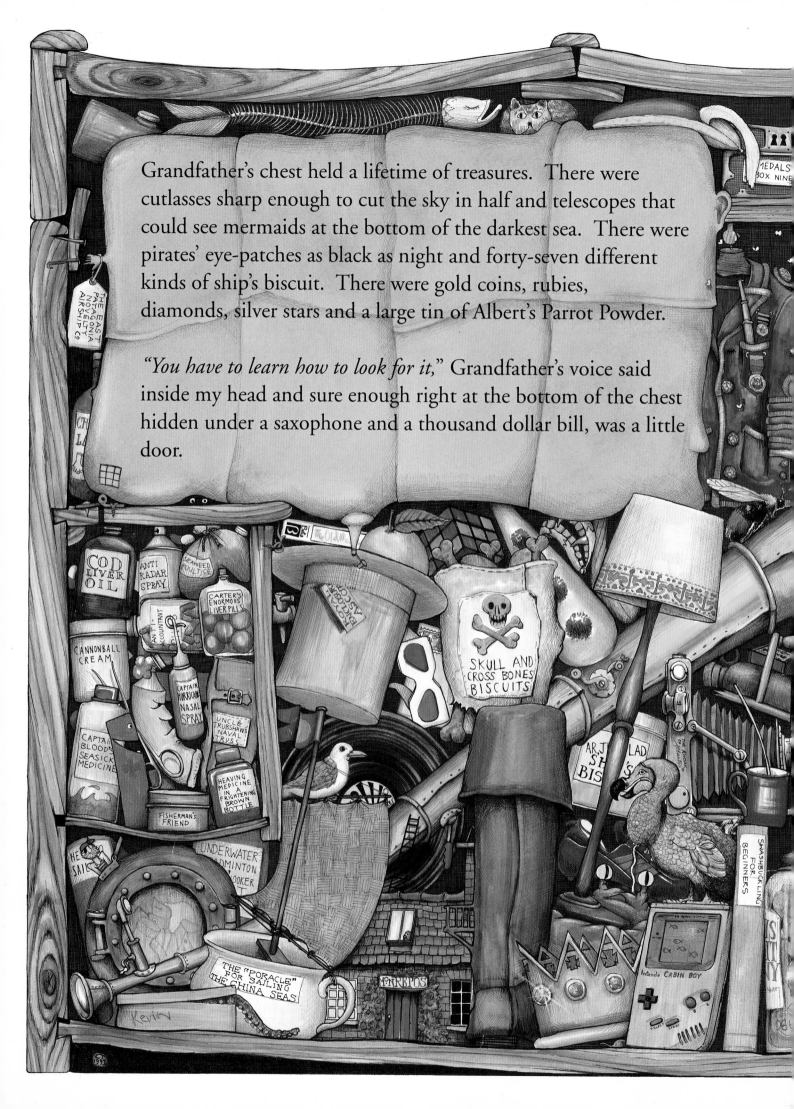

Grandfather's chest held a lifetime of treasures. There were cutlasses sharp enough to cut the sky in half and telescopes that could see mermaids at the bottom of the darkest sea. There were pirates' eye-patches as black as night and forty-seven different kinds of ship's biscuit. There were gold coins, rubies, diamonds, silver stars and a large tin of Albert's Parrot Powder.

"You have to learn how to look for it," Grandfather's voice said inside my head and sure enough right at the bottom of the chest hidden under a saxophone and a thousand dollar bill, was a little door.

And through the door was treasure.

I didn't show anyone what I'd found. They wouldn't believe in Atlantis.

"It's just a silly old man's dream," they would have said.

Grandfather had said that you had to
look at things with your imagination.

"You have to shut your eyes," he said,
"and open your heart. When you can do that
everything you ever wanted will be right in front of you."

I tried to look at everything the way Grandfather had said.

I looked round the room then closed my eyes and tried to see it all inside my head, but everything was muddled up like a dream.

I looked in every dark corner and every book.

I looked on every shelf and in every cupboard.

But all I could see was all I could see.

I had been through every room in the house and found nothing. Once or twice I'd thought I'd seen something out of the corner of my imagination but when I'd opened my eyes and looked it had just been Titanic's feathers falling through the sunlight. Maybe Atlantis *was* just an old man's dream? Or maybe I just couldn't see things the right way? I began to feel very small and lost.

The old parrot tried to fly into the darkness below the stairs but he had grown so bald that he could no longer fly. He fell head over heels down the stone steps and lay squawking at the bottom.

I ran down the steps and picked up the old bird. Through his cold skin I could feel his tiny heartbeat, a minute pulse that had carried him through thirty years of life. There were tears on his chest but I think they were mine. We stood in the darkness both feeling the awful loss of someone we had loved. The darkness grew darker. Eyes open, eyes closed, it was all the same.

And then as we stood there below the house the sun came out.

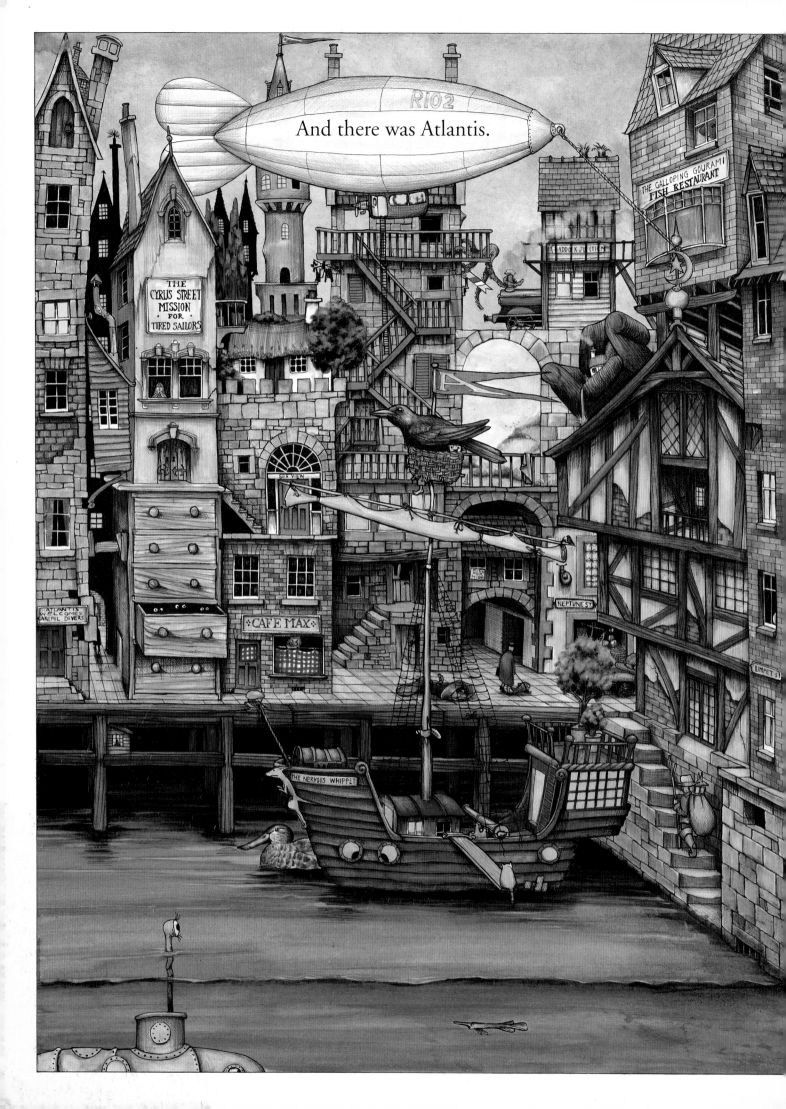

And there was Atlantis.

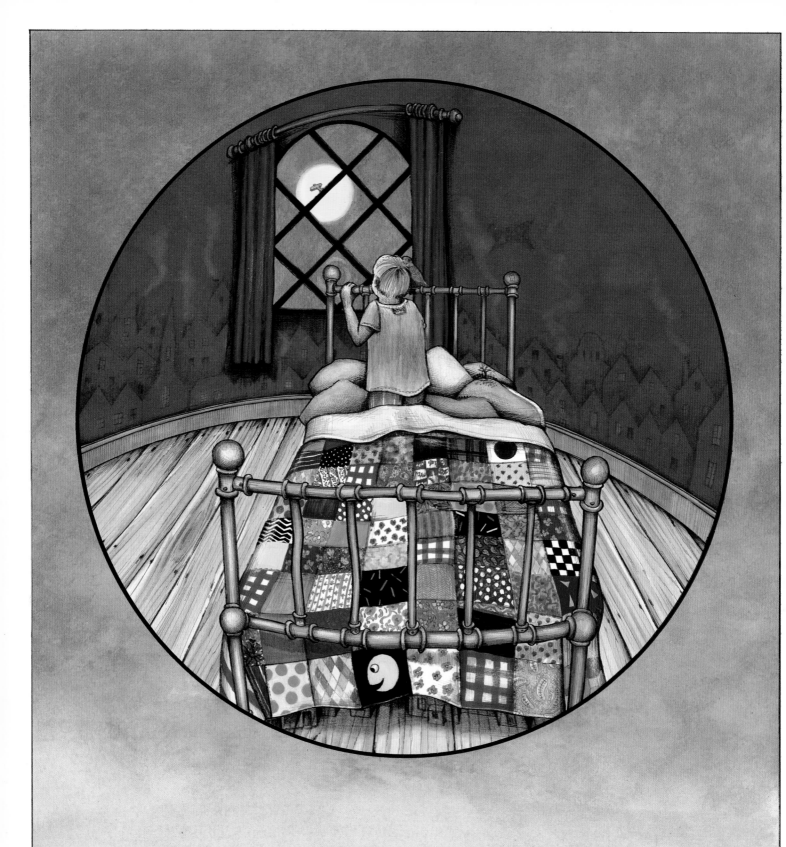

My grandfather had been right. At last I had learned how to
look. I had learned that hopes and dreams are not just inside
your head, and that I could keep Atlantis and Grandfather in my
heart forever.